The Secret of Saying Thanks

Douglas Wood

Illustrated by Greg Shed

Simon & Schuster Books for Young Readers

New York London Toronto Sydney

The world is full of secrets,
gentle, shy things that some people know
and some don't.
The best secrets are the ones that make us happy,
and the best thing about any secret
is sharing it with someone else who wants to know. . . .

Perhaps you'd like to know a secret,
one of the happiest ones of all.
You will surely find it for yourself one day.
You'll discover it all on your own,
maybe when you least expect it.

You might discover the secret at dawn,
a morning like all other mornings.
The sun climbs over the edge of the earth
and begins to fill the world with light and warmth.
It touches your cheek with a golden ray,
and you say softly, simply, "Thanks.
Thank you, sun, for the gift of a new day,
for all its choices and challenges,
for all the beauty that it brings."

Or sometime perhaps you'll notice a flower
as if for the very first time,
and thank it and all of its bright brothers and sisters
for the grace of their blossoms
and the sweetness of their breath,
for coloring your path and reminding you
how easy it can be to smile.

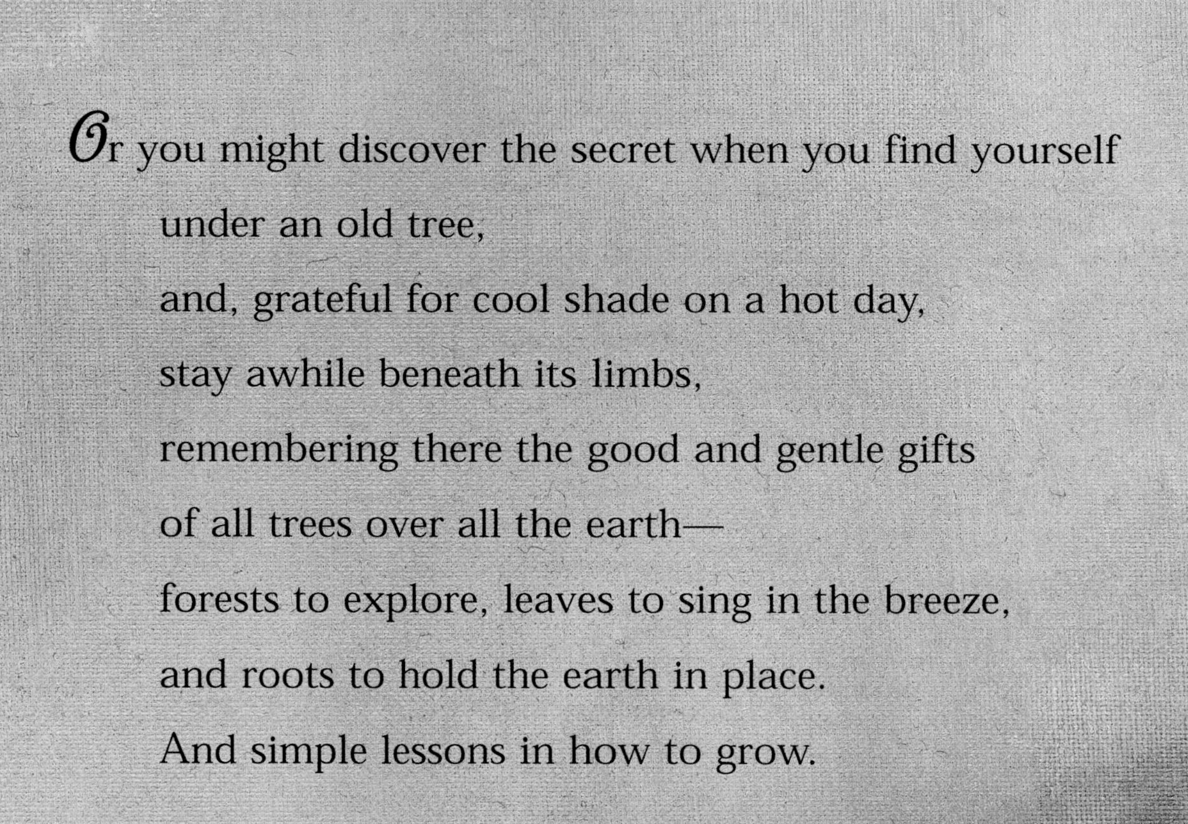

Or you might discover the secret when you find yourself
under an old tree,
and, grateful for cool shade on a hot day,
stay awhile beneath its limbs,
remembering there the good and gentle gifts
of all trees over all the earth—
forests to explore, leaves to sing in the breeze,
and roots to hold the earth in place.
And simple lessons in how to grow.

One long day you may stop to rest
upon a rock—a silent stone
that's been waiting age upon age for someone
to come along and just say, "Thank you.
Thank you, all stones and rocks and pebbles
and hills and mountains.
Thanks for your silence and patience,
for standing still and not changing
in a world so full of noise and speed and change."

You may find the secret when you hear a bird sing
and feel grateful for the gentle music of the skies,
for flash of wing and brightness of feathers,
for the good company of graceful creatures
who dance upon the wind.

And perhaps you'll remember to thank
all creatures
who swim or crawl or creep
or burrow or climb or run;
creatures with fur or feathers,
horns or hooves or scales or shells.
They remind us of the mystery and beauty
of all life, and they save us from a great loneliness
here on our small, blue planet,
sailing among the stars.

And those stars themselves,
tiny, twinkling beams from far, far away,
farther than you can even dream,
that give just enough light for dreaming
or wishing upon.
Don't forget to thank them,
and the soft, shining moon, the night-sun
that helps us to find our way in the dark.

Beneath the moon, the earth's waters are spread with silver;
lakes and rivers, ponds and puddles,
and streams and oceans.
It is the waters that make the magic of life possible.
Perhaps one day, taking a cool drink
or paddling a canoe,
or swimming or splashing in the sun,
you will remember to say, "Thanks.
Thank you, waters, for sweet drinks,
for cool swims and reflecting sunsets,
and for the gift of life itself."

Maybe you'll first find the secret
in your own home,
sitting around a table with people you love,
giving thanks for good food and the good earth
that gave it,
for the many hands that prepared it,
and for family to share it.

Perhaps one day you'll *feel* the secret,
when someone is holding your hand
or kissing away tears
or hugging you close
or reading you a story
or tucking you into bed at night,
and reminding you to say your prayers.

Or it might be in your bedtime prayer itself,
as you say thanks for
sun and moon and stars
and rocks and trees
and flowers and waters
and birds and animals
and all those who love you,
and the love you feel for them.

For here is the secret,

if you've not already guessed it. . . .

The heart that gives thanks is a happy one,

for we cannot feel thankful and unhappy at the same time.

The more we say thanks, the more we find to be thankful for.

And the more we find to be thankful for, the happier we become.

We don't give thanks because we're happy.
We are happy because we give thanks.

To my family, for whom I'm
thankful every day—D. W.

To Arnelle—G. S.

SIMON & SCHUSTER BOOKS FOR YOUNG READERS
An imprint of Simon & Schuster Children's Publishing Division
1230 Avenue of the Americas, New York, New York 10020

Book design by Einav Aviram
The text for this book is set in Sabon.
The illustrations for this book are rendered in gouache.
Manufactured in China
2 4 6 8 10 9 7 5 3
CIP data for this book is available from the Library of Congress.
ISBN-13: 978-0-689-85410-1
ISBN-10: 0-689-85410-2